For Audrey and Will Olson
Thea Wright
Evie and Kate Kranias
Hutton Yankie
and Lenny Franco

The world is yours.
May you find your wings!
—G. E. L.

This book is dedicated
to Katie & Leo, Honey & Maggie,
and especially, to Cheryl.
—M. W.

atheneum

An imprint of Simon & Schuster Children's Publishing Division
1230 Avenue of the Americas, New York, New York 10020
Text copyright © 2013 by George Ella Lyon
Illustrations copyright © 2013 by Mick Wiggins
All rights reserved, including the right of reproduction
in whole or in part in any form.
ATHENEUM BOOKS FOR YOUNG READERS is
a registered trademark of Simon & Schuster, Inc.
Atheneum logo is a trademark of Simon & Schuster, Inc.
For information about special discounts for bulk purchases, please contact
Simon & Schuster Special Sales at 1-866-506-1949
or business @ simonandschuster.com.
The Simon & Schuster Speakers Bureau can bring authors to your live
event. For more information or to book an event, contact the
Simon & Schuster Speakers Bureau at 1-866-248-3049 or
visit our website at www.simonspeakers.com.
Book design by Deb Sfetsios-Conover
The text for this book is set in Rockwell.
The illustrations for this book are rendered digitally.
Manufactured in China
0913 SCP
10 9 8 7 6 5 4 3 2
Library of Congress Cataloging-in-Publication Data
Lyon, George Ella, 1949—
Planes fly! / George Ella Lyon ;
illustrated by Mick Wiggins. — 1st ed.
p. cm.
"A Richard Jackson Book."
Summary: Illustrations and easy-to-read rhyming text celebrate
different kinds of planes, their instruments, what they carry, and
what it is like to go for a flight.
ISBN 978-1-4424-5025-7 (hardcover)
ISBN 978-1-4424-5026-4 (eBook)
[1. Stories in rhyme. 2. Airplanes—Fiction.] I. Wiggins, Mick, ill. II. Title.
PZ8.3.L9893Pl 2013
[E]—dc23   2012030310

PLANES FLY!

by George Ella Lyon

illustrations by Mick Wiggins

 A Richard Jackson Book

atheneum ATHENEUM BOOKS FOR YOUNG READERS   NEW YORK   LONDON   TORONTO   SYDNEY   NEW DELHI

Planes have engines.
Planes have wings
lifted by the air that sings.

Planes fly!

Bi-planes
tri-planes
gotta-love-the-sky planes.

Prop planes
jet planes
how-fast-can-you-get planes.

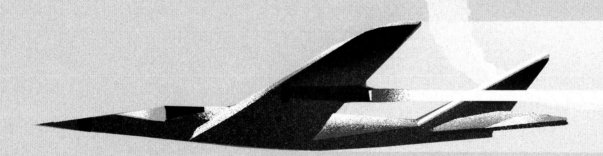

Planes fly!

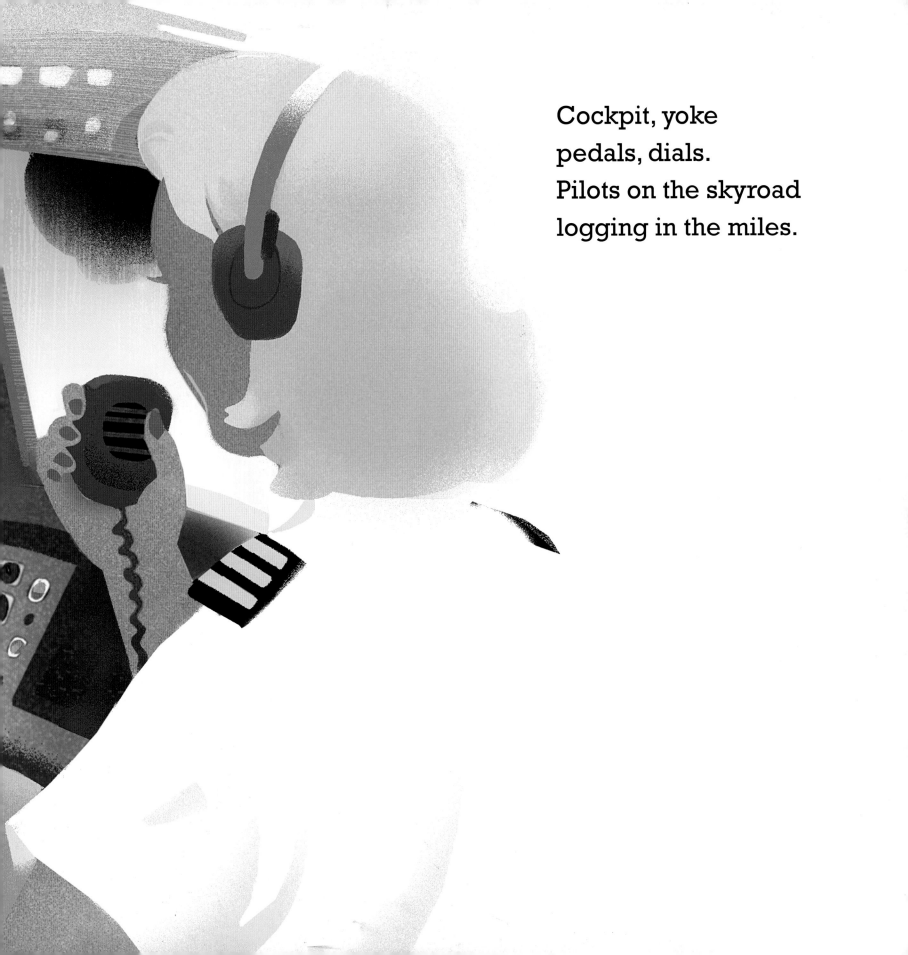

Cockpit, yoke
pedals, dials.
Pilots on the skyroad
logging in the miles.

Rudders, flaps
ailerons, tail
steer the plane
around storms or hail.

Headset, radar
schedule, phone.
Controller in the tower
guiding pilots home

in airplanes
seaplanes
made-for-you-and-me planes.

Hand-built gliders
take-you-for-a-riders.

Big air buses
room-for-all-of-us-es.

Planes fly!

Planes towing banners.
Planes skywriting.

Some loop-the-looping.
Some firefighting.

Some hold lobsters,

racehorses, too.

Some hold the President!
Some hold you!

Fasten your seat belt.
Stow your stuff.

Feel wheels bounce
when the runway's rough.

Watch out the window.
Trees rush past.
Feel the nose lift—
airborne at last!

Planes fly!

Climb through clouds
heading for blue—
just like a bird.
Air holds you

above towns and rivers.

Find them on a map.

Eat a little snack.

Plane noses down
tilts in the wind.

Wheels touch tarmac.
Flight's at an end.

Planes land.

Back on the ground
now you've found
you're a real flier

a take-to-the-skyer

a sleep-on-the-winger
a see-everythinger.

World's mighty big
but there's just one sky
and it's yours to travel.